PETER'S CHAIR

EZRA JACK KEATS

PETER'S CHAIR

PUFFIN BOOKS

For Joan Roseman

Peter stretched as high as he could.
There! His tall building was finished.

CRASH! Down it came.
"Shhhh!" called his mother.
"You'll have to play more quietly.
 Remember, we have a new baby in the house."

Peter looked into his sister Susie's room.
His mother was fussing around the cradle.
"That's my cradle," he thought,
"and they painted it pink!"

"Hi, Peter," said his father.
"Would you like to help paint sister's high chair?"
"It's my high chair," whispered Peter.

He saw his crib and muttered,
"My crib. It's painted pink too."
Not far away stood his old chair.
"They didn't paint that yet!" Peter shouted.

He picked it up and ran to his room.

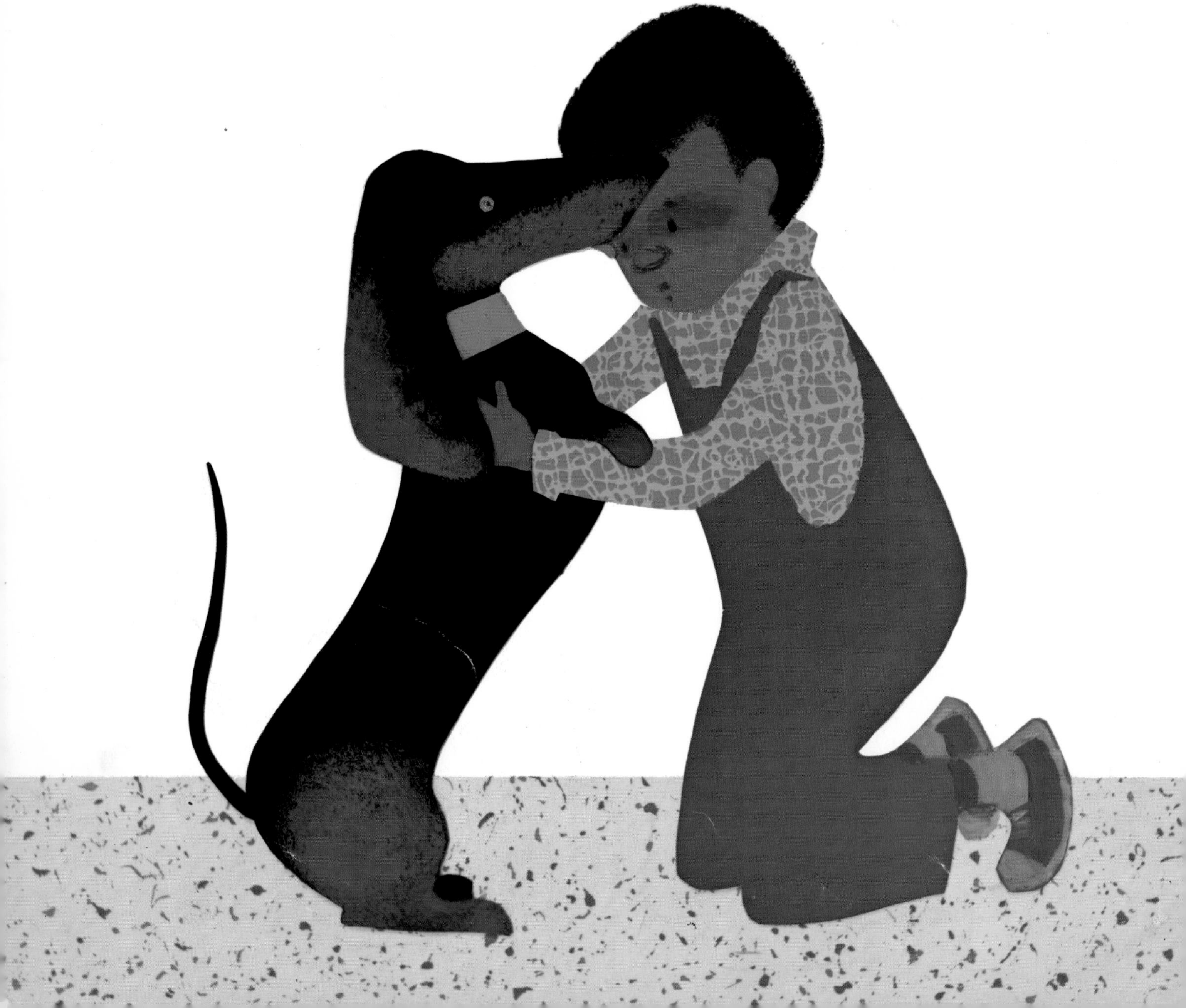

"Let's run away, Willie," he said.
Peter filled a shopping bag
with cookies and dog biscuits.
"We'll take my blue chair, my toy crocodile,
and the picture of me when I was a baby."
Willie got his bone.

They went outside and stood in front of his house.
"This is a good place," said Peter.
He arranged his things very nicely
and decided to sit in his chair for a while.

But he couldn't fit in the chair. He was too big!

His mother came to the window and called,
"Won't you come back to us, Peter dear?
We have something very special for lunch."
Peter and Willie made believe they didn't hear.
But Peter got an idea.

Soon his mother saw signs that Peter was home. "That rascal is hiding behind the curtain," she said happily.

She moved the curtain away.
But he wasn't there!

"Here I am," shouted Peter.

Peter sat in a grown-up chair.
His father sat next to him.
"Daddy," said Peter, "let's paint
the little chair pink for Susie."

And they did.

PUFFIN BOOKS
Published by the Penguin Group
Penguin Putnam Books for Young Readers, 345 Hudson Street,
New York, New York 10014, U.S.A.
Penguin Books Ltd, 27 Wrights Lane, London W8 5TZ, England
Penguin Books Australia Ltd, Ringwood, Victoria, Australia
Penguin Books Canada Ltd, 10 Alcorn Avenue, Toronto, Ontario, Canada M4V 3B2
Penguin Books (N.Z.) Ltd, 182-190 Wairau Road, Auckland 10, New Zealand

Penguin Books Ltd, Registered Offices: Harmondsworth, Middlesex, England

First published in the United States of America by Harper & Row, 1967
Published by Viking and Puffin Books, members of Penguin Putnam Books for Young Readers, 1998

15 17 19 20 18 16 14

LIBRARY OF CONGRESS CATALOGING-IN-PUBLICATION DATA
Keats, Ezra Jack.
Peter's chair / Ezra Jack Keats
p. cm.
Summary: When Peter discovers his blue furniture is being painted
pink for a new baby sister, he rescues the last unpainted item, a
chair, and runs away.
ISBN 0-670-88064-7.—ISBN 0-14-056441-1 (pbk.)
[1. Chairs—Fiction. 2. Babies—Fiction. 3. Brothers and sisters—Fiction.] I. Title
PZ7.K2253Pe 1998 [E]—dc21 97-48302 CIP AC

Printed in Hong Kong